the Blushful Hippopotamus

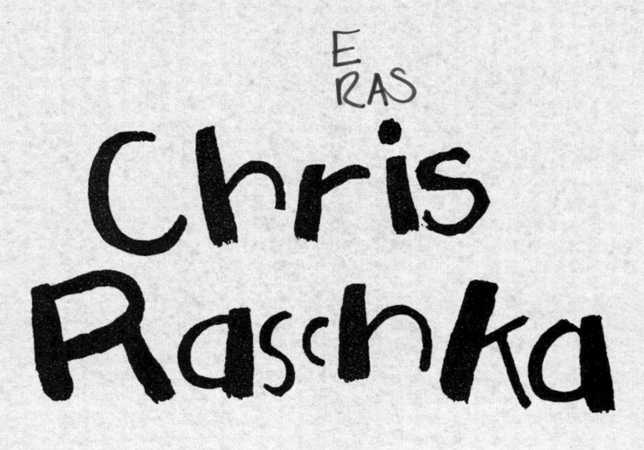

Chris Raschka

Orchard Books New York

Orchard Books • 95 Madison Avenue • New York, NY 10016

Manufactured in the United States of America
Printed by Barton Press, Inc.
Bound by Horowitz/Rae
Book design by Chris Raschka
The text of this book is hand lettered.
The illustrations are watercolor with india ink and oil sticks.

1 2 3 4 5 6 7 8 9 10

Library of Congress Cataloging-in-Publication Data
Raschka, Christopher.
The blushful hippopotamus / Chris Raschka.
p. cm.
"A Richard Jackson book"—Half t.p.
Summary: Though Roosevelt the hippopotamus's sister teases him because he blushes a lot, his best friend helps him feel better about himself.
ISBN 0-531-09532-0. — ISBN 0-531-08882-0 (lib. bdg.)
[1. Hippopotamus—Fiction. 2. Brothers and sisters—Fiction. 3. Blushing—Fiction.] I. Title.
PZ7.R18148Bl 1996 [E]—dc20 95-51562

for B.F.T.

I am the blushful hippopotamus

or so my sister sometimes calls me now.

If I fall down, she likes to call me that.

Darn that sister! She makes me mad, you know.

She says, "Roosevelt" (yes, this is my name),

"are you blushing again, baby brother?"

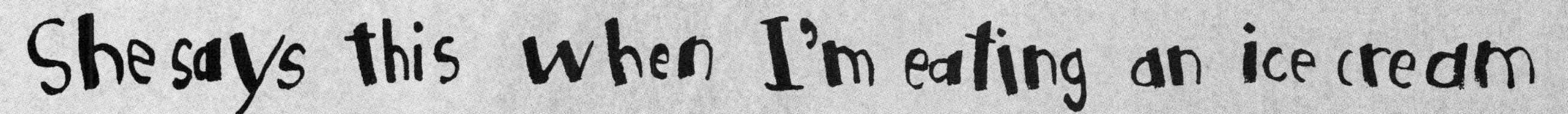

She says this when I'm eating an ice cream

with my friend Lombard, my best friend, Lombard.

"You are a blushful hippopotamus!"

she says, when I'm just having a little

trouble with my bike.

"Are you blushing again, baby brother?"

she asks, when I'm working on my counting.

She says, "You are a blushful hippo baby!"

When I'm trying to think of the right name.

Darn that sister!

"Lombard, <u>am</u> I a blushful hippopotamus?"

Lombard says,

"Roosevelt, a hopeful hippopotamus is what you are."

That's absurd.

Lombard says,

"A mindful hippopotamus,
this is you, too."

Applesauce!

My friend says,

"A thoughtful hippopotamus is who is you."

It is to laugh.

And he says,

"A skillful hippopotamus
is what it is you are."

Pish posh.

Lombard says,

"A wonderful hippopotamus
are you, are you, are you!"

Pooh.

"Thank you, Lombard."